Grandmas Are Lovely

For Olly, Tommy, and Benny —M. C.

For my supportive parents, my husband, John,
and for grandmas living near and far —N. H.

Henry Holt and Company
Publishers since 1866
Henry Holt® is a registered trademark of Macmillan Publishing Group, LLC.
120 Broadway
New York, New York 10271
mackids.com

Library of Congress Cataloging-in-Publication Data is available
ISBN 978-1-250-81653-5

Our books may be purchased in bulk for promotional, educational, or business use.
Please contact your local bookseller or the Macmillan Corporate and Premium Sales Department
at (800) 221-7945 ext. 5442 or by email at MacmillanSpecialMarkets@macmillan.com.

First published in Australia in 2020 by Scholastic Australia
First U.S. edition, 2022

Printed in China by RR Donnelley Asia Printing Solutions Ltd.,
Dongguan City, Guangdong Province

1 3 5 7 9 10 8 6 4 2

Grandmas Are
Lovely

Written by **Meredith Costain**

Illustrated by **Nicolette Hegyes**

GODWINBOOKS

Henry Holt and Company
New York

Grandmas are lovely.

They're joyful and sweet.

And when you are with them,

each day is a treat.

Grandmas are patient
and thoughtful and kind.

The very best playmates

that you'll ever find.

Grandmas are chirpy
and cheery and bright.

They sing funny songs
and bring gifts that delight.

Grandmas are fearless,
courageous, and smart.

They'll love and protect you
with all of their heart.

Grandmas are cuddly
with arms that hug tight.

They wrap you in dreams

when they kiss you good night.

My grandma's so special.

I tell her each day,

I love and adore her . . .

. . . in every way.